Just Like Me!

Adam Relf

STERLING

New York / London
www.sterlingpublishing.com/kids

The rocks started to shake…with laughter! The
rattlesnake was so surprised that he slithered off.
One by one the rocks unrolled themselves. And
as Arlo watched, each rock became an armadillo!
His cousins had been hiding from him all along.

Now Arlo felt very scared. "I really wish there was someone around to help me," he whimpered.

But then something strange happened.

Suddenly, there was a HISSSS
and a terrible rattle.

"Stop pulling my tail!" said a rattlesnake.
Arlo immediately fell back in surprise.

"I thought you were an armadillo!" he sa

"Well, you made a BIG mistake!"
hissed the snake.

Arlo was all alone again.

"I've found animals with scaly heads, pointy ears, and knobbly shells, but they weren't at all like me. And they weren't nice to me either. Where could all my cousins be?"

Then he saw a long bony tail.

"It's an armadillo for sure!" Arlo cried out. "I've got you now!"

Arlo pulled and pulled, and the tail got longer and longer. He must have found his biggest cousin!

"I'm not an armadillo," the tortoise exclaimed.
"And you're too noisy. Please leave me alone!"
"Oops!" thought Arlo.

But it was a tortoise, not one of Arlo's cousins. The tortoise was scared by Arlo's shouting, so he disappeared inside his shell and refused to come out.

As he climbed up a hill, Arlo saw an animal with a big knobbly shell on its back. It looked just like Arlo's shell.

"I hope it's an armadillo!" he thought, and started to run after him.

"Hellooooo!" he shouted.

But all he found was a small brown rabbit.

"You're not an armadillo!" he said.

"No, I'm not!" said the rabbit. "But come and help me dig this hole."

Arlo joined in the digging, but the rabbit dug too fast and covered him in dirt. Muddy, hot, and grumpy, Arlo scrambled out of the hole and walked away.

He walked on until he saw two pointy ears nearly hidden behind a pile of earth. They looked just like Arlo's ears.

"This must be my cousin digging a hole!" he thought. "I'm coming in!" he called, and took a running jump.

But to Arlo's surprise, three young alligators grinned back at him.

"You're not armadillos," said Arlo. "But maybe we can be friends."

The alligators gnashed their teeth and flicked their tails.

"You're too rough for me!" said Arlo.

"Oh, please stay!" said the alligators. "We'll have lunch together."

But Arlo was already on his way.

Arlo walked along the river until he saw three funny scaly heads just peeping out of the water. They looked just like Arlo's head.

"Ah ha!" he shouted. "Three of my armadillo cousins! Come out and play!"